D0369682

A First-Start Easy Reader

This easy reader contains only 56 different words, repeated often to help the young reader develop word recognition and interest in reading.

Basic word list for *Betsy the Babysitter:*

I	baby	read
am	babysitter	play
a	Betsy	hide
is	little	under
my	girl	behind
me	find	seek
we	finds	sometimes
and	to	rug
but	she	love
big	gets	chimney
this	looks	house
the	with	rider
then	mother	tired
when	sister	still
say	horse	books
not	horsey	games
up	tries	dolls
make	always	pictures
	good	night

Betsy

the Babysitter

Written by T. Crawford

Illustrated by Judith Fringuello

Troll Associates

This is Betsy.

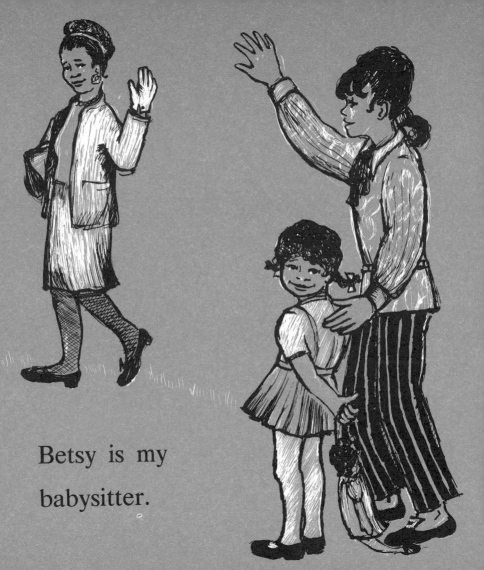

Betsy is my
babysitter.

I am not
a baby.

I am
a little
girl.

But Betsy is still my babysitter.

We read books.

We make dolls.

We play games.

Sometimes, we play

hide and seek. I hide

and Betsy tries to find me.

She looks under the rug.

Behind pictures.

Up the chimney.

But Betsy always finds me.

I love to play with Betsy!

When we play house,
I am the mother,

and Betsy is the baby.

When we play "horsey,"

I am

the rider

and

Betsy is the horse.

But sometimes Betsy gets tired.

Then
I say
good night.

"Good night, Betsy."

I
love
Betsy.

Betsy the babysitter is my big sister!